Written by Emily Gale
Illustrated by Mike Byrne

First published by Parragon in 2010

Parragon
Queen Street House
4 Queen Street
Bath BA1 1HE, UK

ISBN 978-1-4075-9507-8

Printed in China

# JUST JOSIE 7

### and the lucky number!

## PaRragon

Bath · New York · Singapore · Hong Kong · Cologne · Delhi · Melbourne

Zac mainly likes to show off about his dog. Buster.

Watch this, Josie!

shouts Zac over the fence.

"Isn't that the smartest
thing you've ever seen?"
says Zac. "Nyah-nyah! Bet
you wish YOU had a dog."

# "It's not fair!"

Josie yells and runs up to her bedroom . . .

. . . and grabs her paper and pens.

DEEP BREATH,
COUNT TO TEN.
JOSIE'S GOT A
BIG IDEA AGAIN.

I might not have
a dog, but i DO have
a little sister. I'll show
Zac what smart tricks
REALLY are.

She writes Zac a note.

Dir Zac,
My sista is better
than yor dog.
I will show you
tmorro.    JosiE.

Josie puts the note through Zac's fence and hurries back inside to start her BIG Idea.

PROJECT LILY

"Okay, Lily, Buster can roll over, sit up and beg, and 'high five.' You can do all of those things too, but it has to be BETTER than that. It has to be SMART. Say the alphabet," says Josie.

Lily takes a deep breath
and talks really loud and fast.

a b c d e f g h i j k
j j j k j j j . . . k . . .

And then she stops.
"The alphabet has too many
letters," says Josie.
"I need to find something
easier for you."

"Lily, count to ten," says Josie. Lily starts to spin round and round.

"One . . . two . . . three . . . four . . . five . . . six . . . "

Lily keeps spinning, but she stops counting.

"Keep going!" says Josie.

"EIGHT
NINE
TEN!"

Lily falls in a heap giggling.

"You missed seven! Try again—this has to be PERFECT to teach that silly old Zac a lesson."

A note has come under the kitchen door.
It is from Zac.

Josie,

Evryone knows that dogs do betta trix.

U R A Sor looza.

Zac

Josie CANNOT let Zac think that he can teach better tricks than her. She is going to teach Lily how special and important the number seven is. "Seven days in the week," she says.

Monday,
Tuesday,
Wednesday,
Thursday,
Friday,
Saturday,
Sunday.

Lily sticks out her tongue.
"Seven colors in the rainbow."
says Josie.
"Red. yellow. pink. green
purple. orange. and blue.
Now you try."

Lily grins. "One. two. three. four. five. six. eight. nine. ten!"

Then she burps.

Josie picks up her xylophone stick.
"Seven notes in a scale." she says.
and then Josie sings:

"DO"

re, mi, fa, so, la, ti."

Lily claps for
her big sister.

"Say seven.
SE-VEN,"
says Josie.
Lily shrugs
and says
she's hungry.

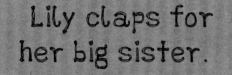

DEEP BREATH,
COUNT TO TEN.
JOSIE'S GOT A
BIG IDEA AGAIN.

"Zac gives Buster
doggy treats," she says.
"I just need to find
some Lily treats!"

Josie gives Lily three chocolate bars
and four chocolate cookies.
"Seven treats, Lily!"

Lily eats
them really
fast.

She has
chocolate
oozing
out of the
corners
of her
mouth.

She still won't
say seven.

That night Lily watches her big sister
button up her pajamas.

"I'm not speaking
to you." says Josie.
"You ruined
my Big Idea."

Josie cuddles
up to Duck and
won't give Lily
a kiss good night.

But later, in the dark, Josie gets a bad feeling all over. She creeps across the floor to where her little sister is sound asleep. Josie loves the way that Lily smells like cupcakes when she's cozy in bed.

"You're still the best sister in the world," she whispers. "Even if you're no good at tricks." Josie gives her sister some good-night kisses.

"Kisses for your
eyes—one. two.
Nose—three.
Mouth—four.
Cheeks—five. six.
Night-night. Lil."
Then Josie tiptoes away.

And a very sleepy voice says. "Seven."
"What did you say?" says Josie.
"Seven." whispers Lily.

One two three four
five six SEVEN
eight nine ten.

Josie climbs into bed with her little sister.
"I don't care what Zac thinks," says Josie.
"You really are BETTER than a dog."

And Lily falls fast asleep in her big sister's arms.